DARE to Write
in a FLASH

Lynn
Life is a
dare

Love Kim

DARE
to Write in a
FLASH

Learning and Fine Tuning
the Art of Writing

Toni Kief

The Writers Cooperative of the Pacific Northwest
Seattle, Washington 2018

The Writers Cooperative of the Pacific Northwest
Seattle, Washington 2018

ISBN: 9781731244741

Toni Kief's website: www.tonikief.com

Cover design: Heather McIntyre, www.coverandlayout.com
Cover photos: Typewriter © Devanath, Pixabay

Interior design: Heather McIntyre, www.coverandlayout.com

This book is dedicated to the
Writers Kickstart of Snohomish, WA.
Struggling together for longer than expected.

Special Thanks to Celena D. Dunivent.
Thanks for your encouragement and the
excitement of your Flash stories.

DARE to Write
in a FLASH

− Contents −

Introduction:	From Me to You	1
FLASH 1:	Fame and Fortune in 5 Steps	5
FLASH 2:	No Room Big Enough	9
FLASH 3:	Walk-Ins Welcome	13
FLASH 4:	Anonymous No More	15
FLASH 5:	Genius	19
FLASH 6:	Led by a Dark Star	23
FLASH 7:	This Was Not the Plan	25
FLASH 8:	The Noise in My Kitchen	27
FLASH 9:	The Story Speaks	29
FLASH 10:	A Dream Remembered	33
FLASH 11:	Bus Stop	37
FLASH 12:	Unfastened a Mind in Heartbeat Time	39
Work Section 1:	Kickstarter Writer Prompts	41
Work Section 1:	Now Write Your Story	45
FLASH 13:	Gazing Out to Sea	49
FLASH 14:	Edge of the Alphabet	51
FLASH 15:	Life Three Acts	53
FLASH 16:	Master of His Universe	57
FLASH 17:	It's the Trip	59
FLASH 18:	Bucket List	63

FLASH 19:   Hemingway Walks into a Bar   67

FLASH 20:   Letter to the Author   71

FLASH 21:   The Calling   75

FLASH 22:   Mystery of Night   77

FLASH 23:   Too Much Magic   79

FLASH 24:   Trudging Toward the Horizon   81

Work Section 2   Kickstarter Writer Prompts   83

Work Section 2: Now Write Your Story   87

FLASH 25:   Delusions in Ink   91

FLASH 26:   Cheap at Half the Price
                 (All prices should be
                 adapted for inflation)   93

FLASH 27:   The Stranger   97

FLASH 28:   Paper and Pen   101

FLASH 29:   Possessed   103

FLASH 30:   Right, Wrong and Sideways   105

FLASH 32:   The Family Has a Poet   107

FLASH 33:   Don't Get Comfortable   109

FLASH 34:   After Dusk   111

FLASH 35:   3AM Saturday   113

FLASH 36:   Preheat to 425   115

FLASH 37:   Run-Drop-Hide   117

Work Section 3: Kickstarter Writer Prompts   119

Work Section 3: Now Write Your Story   123

Other works by Toni Kief   127

About the Author   129

– INTRODUCTION –

From Me to You

I approached retirement with no idea what I wanted to be when I grew up. I didn't pick up the creative pen until I was sixty years old. It is important to realize that when I took English, Agatha Christie was still alive. Here I sat with a High School diploma and twenty- three years of community college required courses (which includes six years of yoga). Not a single writing class on my resume. I'll admit, I had written a couple of pieces that were poetry-like. What a surprise to learn poetry has rules; I claim they don't always apply to the poet. In the days contemplation, I was forced to realize how little I knew.

At a fortuitous moment, an acquaintance of mine said, (and this is an exact quote) "I want to write more."

As any good friend would do, I wanted to encourage him. So, my answer was, "If you write – I'll write." Unplanned time had passed, now retired with time to invest, I fulfilled my promise. I have three completed novels, a fourth in motion, short story compilations and two more books in the hopper. I spoke with a few local authors, and the familiar tale was that they often started as a child. They claim that they knew as soon as they were capable of holding a #2 pencil. I searched for support and encouragement.

Unbeknownst to me, I have prepared. I've been a reader ever since Fun With Dick and Jane. That practice provided unacknowledged tools. My next decision, maybe one of the best, was to join a writing group. Unsure where to go, I learned of MeetUp.com. They offer groups of all kinds darn near everywhere. I found Writer's Kickstarter. We met at a deli, talked, bragged and wrote. We eventually began writing Flash Fiction pieces based on prompts. As the group grew we placed a limit of five hundred words. The writing exercises taught so much on using the best words and trusting your readers to participate. The readers' imagination fills in many details. You need to describe, but don't be a maniac. No one wants to know "he had intense, sparkling, blazing blue eyes" thirty times. Leave some of those cursed adverbs in the delete pile and trust your reader's imagination. If you need to add a descriptive to a verb, search for a better verb.

The steps to become a writer:
1. Read books
    a. Big books and small books.
    b. Long books, and short books.
    c. Books in genres you like.
    d. Books in genres you have avoided.
    e. Read books similar to what you want to write.
    f. Learn, don't imitate or copy.
2. Use a thesaurus and a dictionary (digital or print) and use them until they are tattered.

3.   Set manageable goals.
   a. If you set a small goal, it is easier to start, and you are rewarded with much more.
   b. I also reward myself when I accomplish the goal. It started being $1 a day, but that didn't work, because I knew where the money was kept. Now, I work to earn quality English Breakfast tea. If I don't put in a serious effort, I have to drink the 2 for $5 bargains from the grocery store.

4.   Follow the old advice: butt in chair, pen in hand.
   a. Outline or not depending on how you create. Keep track of characters and details that you can refer to when necessary.
   b. I have a character spreadsheet clipped to my office lamp and a giant whiteboard on the wall.
   c. A warmer for tea, coffee or beverage of choice. (A little spoiler. Nothing worse than a tepid hot drink or a warm cold one to break your concentration).
   d. Get the first draft on the page. Don't edit, don't judge. Write.
   e. Once finished go back and reread, watch for repeated phrases and slangs that can confuse readers.
   f. Read it out loud. You catch things your silent brain has hidden from you.

g. Edit your manuscript after it's written.

h. You need someone else to read it after you have been through the document multiple times and are convinced it is perfect. (Beta readers, not sisters, etc.)

i. Find a good editor.

j. You don't have to accept all edits but consider them and be open.

5. Don't forget: all stories have been told before. It's up to you to create something with originality and the brilliant flair only you can supply.

6. One more time—read.

7. Okay, and review works by others. We all need the input and encouragement.

GET BUSINESS CARDS AND TAKE ON THE TITLE OF WRITER/AUTHOR ADD IT TO YOUR NAME TAGS.

– FLASH 1 –

Fame and Fortune in 5 Steps

1. You have an original story rolling around in your brain, been there for years. It's time to write. Go to Target; buy a large spiral notebook, pens, paperback dictionary, and binder. While there check out the plastic picnicware and try on shoes that match nothing. Buy sandwich supplies and water bottle; you will need these while penning the best story since Steinbeck died. Head home inspired and ready.

2. Driving past Best Buy ponder the pros of writing your inspiration on your computer, editing will be easier. Make U-turn to purchase a zip drive to protect your tale of humor and quiet wisdom. Check out the $5 movie bin, put back Ernest goes to Camp, you didn't like that movie in 1987, and it is still stupid. While bent over looking at a bug zapper, Greg, the teenaged clerk will offer help. Ask him where they keep the zip drives, returning

to the task. Turning to walk towards the rear of the store where he pointed, stop to test the 3 D glasses and watch dolphins frolic in the early mist on a 78 - inch color TV. Proceed through home entertainment towards the zip drives. Price printers; you will need one for the profound inspiration of a life well lived. Play Angry Birds on sample tablet, and gasp at the price. A six-gigabyte zip drive is $39.99. When did that happen? Use two credit cards to pay for a laptop with a free printer. Much better investment than a zip drive, because you can work anywhere and produce the next New York Times break out hit while at Starbucks.

3. Set the alarm for 6:00 a.m., you know your muse is sharpest in the mornings. Hit snooze, and again at 6:30, 7, 7:30. Rise at 8:30 sharp, to set up the laptop, feed cats, clean litter box, eat cold English muffin. Take a shower, and dress comfortably. Wear raggedy sweater that would have made Sylvia Plathe giggle. Return to Best Buy for a wireless router so you can connect to the internet, for access to Thesarus.com. This will be a mandatory tool for your in-depth treatise on Puritan politics. Your brother calls to meet at Denny's and use free beverage coupon that's due to expire. Stop at Half Price books spend 2 hours 45 minutes

and $127 for cookbooks, writers guide and a mystery series by Tony Hillerman. Immediately, upon your return home, connect to X-Finity Direct TV and watch Ernest Goes to Camp, cost $2.99, savings of $2.01. Read Coyote Waits until 12:11 a.m.

4. Set the alarm for 7 a.m. to start when you are fresh. 7:40, open laptop, check email and post status on Facebook about starting the next great saga of bravery, struggle, improbable science, and deception in medieval Scotland. 2:45 p.m. sign off Facebook and go back to word document. Spend three hours on 500 - word prompt based on garlic for Writer's Kickstart meeting.

5. Call into work at 6:45 a.m. beg for a personal day. Open word doc and type, *It was stormy on that dark night...*

– FLASH 2 –
No Room Big Enough

She lies naked and silent on a dirty mattress with one thin blanket. Her skin has paled and her muscles wasted as she continues to breathe one inhalation at a time waiting for death. The only difference between night and day is the sounds upstairs; a life where she plays no part. For a while she tried to keep track of time, but it only made things worse, knowing which days he would turn on the overhead light.

All hope had deserted her a long time ago, but this day was different. Something new to the blackness someone else may not have noticed, but she had nothing else to do but search the shadows. A single dot of light appeared on the ceiling. Over the hours it crept down the wall and then disappeared near the cage where she could almost touch it. And she decided to live another day.

On the third morning, she imagined where the sunlight had been through the night. On the tenth day, she visualized it warming rice paddies in China. She could smell the new growth of tiny shoots and the wetness of the water flooding the rows in the fields. The brilliance of her sunbeam encourages the plants to grow, and she would hoe until her back aches. She begins to stand up and move her arms and legs, the chains transform into farming tools.

After a while, she harvests the rice and fills canvas bags with the tiny grains of her labor. As the light kisses the ceiling, she loads Apoo, her donkey, and begins to walk. With the sunbeam, they traversed deserts and into the mountains of Nepal. She walks for days, finding grass and water for the cantankerous beast, as they continue the journey.

They arrive in India, and she unloads the rice and sells it for golden coins. She buys a blanket for Apoo and a carrot they can share. Instead of going back to China, they decide to continue west. Weeks go by in the noisy and colorful land. She tours the countryside and on the days the light doesn't appear they visit cities and towns. Surrounded by foreign music and the smells of exotic food prepared in the street.

The only plan was west when they enter Pakistan and climbed mountains she had never imagined existed. As the angle of the light changes and there are more dark days, the duo enter Afghanistan. Weeks pass with quiet, lovely women who teach her about courage in their single room homes. She smells cooking oil and she honors the challenge of feeding children in times of war.

The shaft of light becomes brighter as they travel to Turkey. She smiles remembering the day she loaded Apoo on a fishing boat to travel to Greece. He is not a seafaring beast. The brilliant turquoise water calls, but knowingly, the twosome continue west.

Slowly her journey continues, confident everything changes. Days, weeks and months pass steadily as she gets stronger. Vicariously she lives a full life and rests with the hope of another day. She will not only survive her imprisonment, but she thrives. Margaret takes back her name and knows there is no room big enough to contain her, not now, not ever, and freedom will return when they reach Paris.

– FLASH 3 –

Walk-Ins Welcome

In ancient Greece, the gods are blessed with eternal life. Nine goddesses still haunt Mount Olympus and flit around the earth below. Personified as the Muses. Calliope, metronome for epic poetry, Clio, historical provocateur, Euterpe, inspirator of song, Thalia, top banana of comedy and pastoral poetry, Melpomene, a tragedy trigger, Terpsichore, choreographer of dance, Erato, (can we guess) the muse of love poetry, Polyhymnia, sacred song sponsor, and Urania, supernova of astronomy.

They are an elusive crew, impossible to corner or identify by sight. Not a one of the Muses shows any respect for appointments, sleep, or technology. They seldom travel in a group even though they are sisters from the same mountain village. There is no telling which one will tap you, but she will. I can't give any clues about the form your Muse may take; they are a tricky pack of deities. Their visits aren't preceded by a trumpeted introduction, and often they are just a nagging thought. No one else will hear them arrive or wave when they leave. There is no record of them ever bringing a covered dish, and they run off before you grasp the full intention and find a pen. Your

Muse offers only the slightest suggestion, a whisper, a glance, or a twisted view of the unexpected, and she leaves the details to you. Their voice of creativity actually comes from within, and they present two choices, accept or ignore.

Our job as writers is to grasp the wisp when it appears and wrestle it to a page. My suggestion is to keep paper, pens or recorders with you always. A tablet should be next to the bed, and every night ask to remember your dreams. Make the note, but take the time to allow the ideas to germinate, simmer and boil. Many of the best revelations may sit to the side for years, waiting for the right time. Others will jump out and demand attention. Don't hesitate to start down the wrong path; it may loop back to genius, and maybe not. Spend time with your creativity, visit it, research it, write it repeatedly and help it come to life. Don't judge the motivation; we will let scholars answer the question, they get paid for that. You are allowed to play with the germinating story. Trust in your brilliance to raise it to an art form. Don't question your talent, package the gift of inspiration into the shape that pleases you. Nurture yourself; trust in your ability to give the spark of life that the ideas deserve. Build your personal creative space, and develop the discipline to be there. Be prepared when the Muse sneaks in. Her job is to rattle your day with a thousand possibilities, and it will change your life. She will leave, which is part of the alchemy in the chosen art. You are the magician that can transform the gift.

You have permission to fail, which opens the door wide for the ignition to succeed.

– FLASH 4 –
Anonymous No More

For most of history anonymous was a woman – Virginia Wolfe.

History has been remiss in honoring women. If men made history, it is guaranteed the delicate sex was also there. So many names and triumphs have vanished into the Mrs.

Sofonisba Anguissola was one of the first women, to be allowed art lessons, only because her father was an artist. A 16th-century portraitist, she was praised for her detail, warm colors, and expressive eyes. Michelangelo sent his drawings to her for critique and copying. She was artistically anonymous.

Right after the Mayflower dropped anchor in the Chesapeake Bay, **Susanna White** bore a child. Her husband, William White died in the first year. Susanna was alone with a toddler and a newborn in the Plymouth colony. She wed Edward Winslow months later. As the first bride, she was one of only four adult women who survived to the first Thanksgiving. Her early history is lost, and her story of survival absorbed into myth. History remembers her husbands, but not Susanna. She was nuptially anonymous.

In 1647, **Margaret Brent** of Maryland colony was able to vote as a property owner. She voted twice, the second time for Cecil Calvert, Lord Baltimore. Shortly after, the governor decided it was an oversight and women would not hold the privilege and power of the vote until 128 years later. Disenfranchised anonymous.

Sybil Ludington rode the same night as Paul Revere. She was 15, traveled twice as far, fought off bandits and didn't fall from her horse. She was able to muster the troops in time to face the British. Since her name didn't rhyme, Revere is singularly credited. Independently anonymous.

Women and wives were never strangers to the battlefield. **Mary Ludwig Hays** was at the Battle of Monmouth; she carried pitchers of water to the soldiers. When her husband was killed in the battle, she took over the cannon. She was one of several women who became identified as Molly Pitcher. FYI, Martha Washington traveled with the Revolutionary army. Every battle George was in; she was there. Washing clothes and preparing food. Would we know her name if she wasn't our original - first lady? Anonymous under fire.

Catherine Littlefield Greene did the initial design and with the help of a plantation slave, (whose name has disappeared; another historically neglected representative) developed the cotton gin. Mrs. Greene financed the production and registration, but because women and slaves weren't allowed to hold patents, she asked the student that was lodging on the plantation working as a handyman, Eli Whitney. Eli registered the application, and edited the story, he is honored in classrooms today, and no one discusses Catherine's involvement. Innovatively anonymous.

Annie Jump Cannon was the curator of astronomical photographs at Harvard Observatory. She was astoundingly efficient and was able to classify up to three stars a minute, and Cannon cataloged several hundred thousand stars to the 11th magnitude. She discovered 300 variable stars, in addition to five novae. Astronomically anonymous.

Born in Warsaw on November 7, 1867, the daughter of a secondary-school teacher. She received a general education in local schools and some scientific training from her father. Would we remember **Marie Curie** if Pierre had not complained when her name was omitted from their first Nobel Prize nomination? She received a half prize for physics in 1903 with Pierre, and 1911 a solo prize in Chemistry. Impossible to ignore but radio-active.

The first US Congress met in 1789. One hundred and twenty-eight years later, **Janette Rankin** was the first woman to represent over half of the US population. She was elected three years before she could vote. Women still have not reached parity, but they are working on it. Unequally anonymous, rule changer.

Margaret Knight was one of the most prolific inventors of the 20th century. She started at twelve with a stop action device for industrial looms. One of the machinists Margaret hired to complete her prototype for the flat bottom paper bag machine submitted her design for a patent. After a bitter court battle, she was able to recover her first patent, followed by 87 more. She improved shoe manufacturing, window frames, the spit for skewering meat, and improvement of the rotary engine. Inventively anonymous.

Each of these stories deserves more detail. This is only a tiny tip of the massive amount of forgotten or absorbed history.

The moral of the story – ladies, all together – **ANONYMOUS NO MORE!**

– FLASH 5 –
Genius

Ilsbeth was a good woman never rich, but seldom hungry. There was always unfinished work with the farm and five energetic boys clamoring for attention. There were rare moments that she could immerse herself in silence to steal a few seconds to read. Those precious moments were followed by nagging guilt. Her husband, a pious man, was often away due to his high position. She would blush at her gratitude for his absence.

All girls married young in those days, Ilsbeth was no exception. She started having babies while still a girl; the boys were the only ones strong enough to survive the challenge of infancy. After years her husband learned to accept her passion and turned a blind eye to her thirst for knowledge. She never realized that he also looked forward to the stories she wove for the boys each night. He allowed, even encouraged her to teach his sons to read. Life would have been very different with daughters.

In the years, that was their marriage; his tolerance developed into a private pride of her brilliant mind. Not that he would ever publicly support her thirst, he brought books from his travels, with the excuse of educating his sons. After burying their eighth child, she found a volume of stories hidden, with her work clothes. He never knew how she loved him when she read and reread the flights of fancy.

Through her long life, she would silently rise early and steal to the community well for water. Here is where she would talk with the other ghosts of the predawn dark. The skeleton of humanity, the bones that shape the culture, the women gathered. In stolen hours they shared their lives, sacred secrets and Ilsbeth read to them. They were friends, no sisters, of the heart. In an unspoken collaboration, the women would bring paper for Ilsbeth's stories, usually a scrap and once a whole sheaf. In this union, she wrote their lives in tales of dreams and fancy. She scribbled of their humbled existence and honored the unspoken sacrifices. Each new moon, when the night was the darkest, they burned the stories and watched the sparks rise becoming points of light in the inky void. Each woman believed her life lived in the universal blackness, this way they mattered.

As the sky warmed to welcome the sun, they would scurry back home before the peace was disturbed. Families stirred and breakfast cooked over open hearths, no man ever learned of the sisterhood. This is how the years passed as Ilsbeth watched her boys grow, and eventually leave as educated men. Once they were gone the new books seldom arrived, but every year there would be one more.

She was given the life; she never was allowed to chose. Ilsbeth was an exception. When still a child she had spied during her brother's lessons trying to salve a persistent curiosity. With stolen moments, she placated her need for education. Ilsbeth's name was lost in the passage of time, but many of her stories live on as legend and myth still repeated by a modern world.

Bones crumbled to dust long ago, yet Ilsbeth's star continues to spread radiance and hope further than the small village. The world is still enlightened by scores of her descendants. Each time we look to the darkest morning sky, we can rest assured that the village sisters watch over us all and conspire for the stories to be written.

– FLASH 6 –
Led by a Dark Star

We lay silently pressing our eyelids together trying to keep the daylight at bay. Our minds race with desire and an aching need to describe. We sort through memories and gather private conversations, building a mental catalog of impossibilities and character. Self-imposed to the outside of a society that we pillage for a glimmer of inspiration. Bastardizing and expanding stolen conversations from a grocery line. We ponder and elaborate upon impossibilities and personal angst because we are writers. Some of us start as children, others at a greater age, but it was always there like a dark star tempting us with a purpose and a journey. Cursed with an ache, a need to record we continue to work with no vacations. Our ears are set to a relentless recognizance, our eyes scan and search as we question philosophies and redesign beliefs.

Our unknown and yet familiar faces are in libraries, bookstores, and the bargain tables, devouring words searching and researching. Amazon, Goodreads, Barnes, and Noble memorize our passwords and send us birthday greetings. We scribble snippets in notebooks, margins, on envelopes, bank receipts, cocktail napkins, paper bags never complete, and forever fearful the idea will slip away. Endlessly confident this is the brilliance that will grow into an opus answering a universal riddle. Then we berate ourselves with personal expectations as we dodge the page with a never-ending frustration of eloquence.

Nights are fitful and tortured as if waiting for a devious lover. In silence, we chew on a phrase or a word exploring a start or defining a finish. We longingly work to expose a stranger's soul, in 500 pages. We drive to have our names recognized and our words repeated while we sit in solitude. Describing our pain, our joy, our most private secrets, is never quite good enough. We compose and edit, reread, rewrite, and obsess convinced that it is easy for the others of our ilk. It isn't.

Inspiration is a vicious mistress who haunts and creeps, but when she surfaces, her beauty is like no other. We, the poets, the storytellers, the reporters, the historians, the liars stand a constant vigil ready and willing to disembowel ourselves for an original narrative. We bleed to the page and dream with the midnight star, to write is our punishment and our art. We recognize at a cellular level that "the end" is only the beginning. We are the writers.

– FLASH 7 –

This Was Not the Plan

In my youth, it was a clear path, school, a good job, marry a nice man and raise curly haired children. By this time of my life, I would still be living in the home where we raised the kids, and we buried eleven dogs and seven cats in the back. The house is full of knickknacks gathered over a lifetime and sorely in need of dusting. I share holidays with generations of people who have hints of me on their face. I was to be the one that could recognize boy in a weathered face that I had shared decades of tribulation and stories that still made us laugh. I would be more conservative and he more liberal, balanced in a lifetime of compromise. That is the dream of the Midwest girls of an earlier time.

But in a moment, it changed. The path of security and partnership ended in seconds unrecognizable until the age of remembrance. The path split to another state, another love. Even today, I don't know the real truth of that choice.

Another chapter, a new book, a new decision. I have never been patient, but I have spent a majority of my life waiting. I still look forward and understand if aced with an immediate decision; I will choose the unknown and the mystery of possibility. When faced with a cheater's accusation, I didn't hesitate and turned my back on years of promises. I moved thousands of miles on several occasions, open to trusting the untrustworthy. I believed that someone could make me whole when I was complete all along.

Is it love I reject, or the everyday. I never planned on the life I have made one snap decision at a time. I have few regrets, but at this time of writing, I look back at what if's. I see that I like who I have become, and who I have always been. I have stories with one familiar character, and that is me. I finally learned that sometimes no decision is a choice too. No has power, and there are no mistakes. Every option, each fence jumped, all of the pillows thrown away, brought me here, tonight, to sit and share your brilliance and my cryptic memories. It is a life of inspiration and not regrets that shadow my earliest mornings.

– FLASH 8 –

The Noise in My Kitchen

It started two weeks ago; I bought Mastering the Art of French Cooking at the used bookstore for $3. In my innocence, I flipped through the pages and scanned a couple recipes. The book was beyond my palate, so I closed the cover and removed it to the bookcase. I am the kind of person who buys wine by the box and never has used it in gravy. I pick and spit delicate truffles, with no regard for rarity or price; a mushroom is a mushroom. That evening I settled into my chair for television and an Aunt Jemima breakfast sandwich with a slice of reheated Red Baron pizza, for an impromptu feast.

Late on the same night, as I deeply slept, there was a high-pitched trill emanating from the kitchen. I convinced myself it was a passing train even though I don't live near any tracks. I rolled with a shiver and searched for dreams. Hours pass and the pots began to rattle and tattle; the pans shifted and clanked. I had a sudden urge to braise beef bones into a clear broth and to eat fishes and snails gathered from seas far from home. I arose and wrapped in false bravado I explored. Finding nothing, I went back to bed for a fretful toss and turn until dawn, blaming the uninspired dynamic dinner whose wrappers and crusts still occupied my trash.

Each night since, I search for slumber with a pounding heart and ears probing a tentative silence. Once I find sleep, there is a noise in my kitchen, followed with an enticing aroma I can't identify. After a fortnight of fear and anticipation, I gave up my search, accepting I can never catch the hazy alchemist who prowls my kitchen.

At daybreak, the constant clanking stops and I nap. When I finally struggle forth, I discover a sink full of dishes and a large metal spoon resting near the stove evidence of the nocturnal intrusions. Julia Child haunts my kitchen. She quietly judges me during the day and prowls at night. I accept responsibility for buying the book and dismissing her lessons. Out of desperation, I remove it from the shelves and return it to the kitchen counter where it belongs. I open a page, dust off my ramekins and encounter herbed baked eggs with thyme infused baguettes.

Today I feast, tonight I rest.

– FLASH 9 –

The Story Speaks

The lights were off as he slipped into the spare room. He closed the door behind him, muting the noise of the other guests. The room was completely dark, as he felt along the smooth walls looking for a switch. Fumbling in the blackness, he blindly crept into the room, searching for a chair. He stumbled into a small desk, and there was a reading lamp. Once clicked on he found what he needed. A tablet and a pen.

John leaned back in the desk chair with the hope that this would quiet the voice in his head. He picked up the pen, clicked it multiple times then put the point on the top line on the tablet. "Okay, tell me what you want." And John started to write.

Unaware of his surroundings the story took hold and spilled onto the pages. John had no concept of time or place until sunlight came through the window breaking the spell. Looking around the room, John was surprised as he gathered the pile of papers and left a note on the last blank page, *thank you I'll owe you a tablet*. Making sure he had all of the manuscript, he then doubled checked to be sure the room was tidy.

Walking out and into the living room he saw Janet slouched on the couch. There was no evidence of the party from the night before, and the reflection from the muted television added a surreal light to the dawn. He stood for a moment, watching her sleep and felt the guilt of his negligence. She turned slightly, and her deep brown eyes opened to look back at him. "All done, Johnny?"

"I don't know, when the light came into the room, the voice stopped."

Janet sat up. "Let's go home, and you can tell me about it on the way." She gathered her bag and slipped on her shoes. "Are you hungry?"

John took the clean casserole dish from her, shut off the TV and opened the door. "I hadn't thought about food, but I could eat."

As Janet shut the door, their eyes locked, and in unison, they whispered "Denny's." Within a few minutes, they walked into an almost abandoned restaurant.

Too late for the night owls, and too early for the rest they had a choice of tables. Once seated they ordered, John reached across the table and took her hand. "I need to apologize to you; I feel terrible about leaving the party. I hope you told everyone that I'm an ass who is truly sorry."

With a big smile, Janet shook her head, "I don't have to apologize for you anymore. Your friends understand. Now, you must tell me what you have. I saw the pages you carried out. Is it a book or a story?"

He signed deeply, "I'm not sure, it was writing itself. Everything stopped when the sun rose this morning. So far it was an elderly man named Bartholomew. Sure, that death was near, he decided to walk into the desert planning to never return. He started at sunset but the further he walked the younger he became. His memories and the things he found were stunning. At one point, when he was miles in, he became afraid to get any younger. He was suspicious that if he turned back, everything would return to the frailty and humiliation of old age? Then the morning interfered, and he left.

The server delivered the plates of eggs, before Janet took a bite, she looked at him fondly, "I guess we may have to wait until sunset to learn what he decides."

– FLASH 10 –

A Dream Remembered

After ten thousand tomorrows, a letter arrived, and she could no longer put off dealing with today. She sat by the cold fireplace, once elegant, and now faded much like her beauty. Years of obsession and business reflected as furrows on her once smooth brow. Tears she used so often abandoned her in this moment of unexpected grief. Rhett is dying. Nothing else but brandy and hard living could have brought an end to their long-hostile marriage. She hadn't seen him since he walked out that foggy night in Atlanta. Never divorced, they held each other prisoner in the only way possible, with a marriage contract.

Scarlett knew the truth about herself, but pushed that inconvenience aside, initially for survival and finally just for power. She used her misguided obsession to hold Ashley as a monetary captive, knowing he never loved her. He eventually married an O'Hara, Scarlett's youngest sister, Carreen. She was the one most like Melanie who captured his heart. Scarlett watched the Wilkes family grew and prosper; always scornful of their misplaced honor and gratitude. Justifying her actions with lies and the war, she never failed to prosper. The only comfort

Scarlett embraced was the one that never failed her – money.

Late in the many sleepless nights, Scarlett replayed distant memories of happiness. All joy was wrapped in the veil of childhood or Rhett Butler. There were only two people who ever knew her and loved her regardless of her willful demands. Mammy raised three generations of O'Hara's while forced to neglect her own children. She was buried at Tara in the O'Hara family plot, forever owned. Scarlett ached for the woman's outspoken counsel and comfort, but this path she would have to travel alone. She decided to go for the last goodbye to the only other person that loved her purely.

A boiling resentment resurged with the letter and initiated her trip. She was arrogant with the knowledge that she is the one he turned to at the end. This was to be her final performance, getting the last word and his fortune.

Scarlett didn't plan on the forced meditation of an ocean crossing. Long, silent days with no demands forced her to face her true character. An expected clarity transformed her narrative.

In the shadow of the Eiffel Tower, she prepared for their final moments. Scarlett put aside the excuses and personal agenda to dress for him one last time. She wore green the color of the dress from the barbeque when they met 50 years ago. Green, the color that defined so many happy moments, was an offering of comfort on this day. Scarlett recognized that this was her last chance to drop the façade and replace it with a rare compassion. Scarlett went to

Rhett; she shared his final minutes with no ulterior motive. This was her first unvarnished act of genuine love. This man, the best and the worst of them, the only one to show her what love could be, died in her arms.

Dare to Write in a Flash

– FLASH 11 –

Bus Stop

Like the refrain of an old blues song, Kelly is not a bad man; he just did a bad thing. Running isn't always the cowardly choice, but fear is a powerful motivator. Sorting through his list of mistakes, he ponders if the big one was taking the job or was it hopping a bus to anywhere with Big Eddie's ledger? Either way, there is no turning back.

Stop! How many fictional characters does it take to fill a bus? Working out another escape scenario, I look back to the hundred odd short stories I've written. It becomes evident that I only know one way out of town. I found a single tale with someone arriving by Greyhound, but the love of her life forgot her at the station. So, she jumped the next express and left his sorry excuses.

Is it anonymity my stories crave? Is it the ability to blend in with 50 road weary blank pages that have no desire to share a history? Is it the opportunity to hide in plain sight behind an overweight uniform that never tires, and drives through the dialogue of imagined nights at consistent 55 miles per hour? That could be important for a getaway, but there is a degree of surrender.

Timing is a consistent influence. A bus moves slower than a plane, but there is no need for a Twenty-one-day advance ticket, showing ID to three TSA agents and passing through a metal detector. Even with a train, you have to anticipate the schedule and a particular exposure to bandits leaping from racing horses onto the mail car. At a bus station, you just walk in, plunk down enough money for a ticket and a Mountain Dew and climb aboard. A different destination every seven minutes, hell, you can even get off at a remote stop for a warm breakfast and life change. Monroe did it in Bus Stop.

Romanticism can't be the reason. Last time I rode a bus, I woke up with some toddler's Cheetos in my hair and 175 more miles to a stationary toilet. I must admit I left Tommy Joy three times by bus, and only once by taking his van.

I'm surprised that the levered door of a Trailways bus is my metaphor. Alternatively, is it just a medium to bless the figures of my imagination with a new chapter, a new challenge or a simplistic exit?

– FLASH 12 –

Unfastened a Mind in Heartbeat Time

A species defined by a need to bond we struggle to determine our social order. An unquenchable desire is to communicate, to teach, to learn, to share. Words ramble through our brains as we search for reason in our personal evolution. Even our unconscious dreams fill with words.

Alone we grapple to mark a piece of paper with a variety of strokes, to punch keys, or speaking the sounds searching for perfection. We gravitate to groups to organize and reorganize the words. Wanting enlightenment in our daily frustrations, we try to summarize the complexity of survival with a limited vocabulary of sounds and letters.

With lips, air, and tongue we pronounce them. A combination of hisses and guttural reverberations choke into a phrase we use to describe. Arms flailing and face contorts as we perform them in a futile attempt to share a story. We often move rhythmically to beautify and celebrate words.

Hate and ignorance pummel without charity to degrade and destroy mocking a victim with words.

Thoughtless expressions spoken in jest unfasten a mind, distorting a dream. A simple utterance spoken without thought rewrites a child story of who they could be. The right combination of sounds spoken earnestly will propel the same child to confidence and success.

A musician's private hell illuminates in a lyrical declaration celebrating the need for emotional release. Storytellers report, gossip and bleed in a need to master the page with an elusive narration. Words wrestled into couplets, and abbreviated lines by poets mold the paper markings into a sigh of truth, pain, and just maybe, humor.

With an extraordinary beauty and a devastating power, we are all imprisoned and yet worship the mysticism of words. Be they your first word or your last encircling the myriad in the middle accept the possibility of beauty and don't ever forget the devastating power.

– WORK SECTION 1 –

Kickstarter Writer Prompts

Pick A Number Between 1 and 100
Write approximately 500 words.

1.   Standing Here Naked
2.   I Believe
3.   First Date
4.   When I Was A Child
5.   The Inhuman Condition
6.   Hemingway Walks into A Bar
7.   Broken
8.   Everyone Loves A Monster
9.   Dirty Secrets
10. On Some Level, He Knew It Was Wrong
11. Finding Your Voice
12. The Jury Is In
13. Tarot Cards
14. Roles
15. Finding the Beauty
16. Groups of Five
17. Shoes
18. First and Main
19. Cookies and Curtains

20. Airstream Trailer
21. Half-Empty Can of Kerosene
22. Decomposing Alligator Snout
23. One Sousaphone
24. Mannequin – Missing Its Head and Dressed in Swim Trunks
25. It Was an Accident
26. Too Much Magic
27. Here I Am Again
28. Ohio
29. A Character from Literature
30. An Albatross
31. In a Class Alone
32. A Trip to Mars
33. That's Rich
34. I Like Having A Choice
35. Good Housekeeping
36. Don't Eat the Purple Ones
37. She's Off Her Medication
38. Deep into The Mystic
39. The Boy Beside the Mailbox
40. Who Will Save The Princess?
41. Walking on The Edge of The Alphabet
42. Two Camels and A 45
43. A Watch That Doesn't Tell Time
44. Nestled in The Corner of The Attic
45. Stress, Taxes, Surgery and A Birthday
46. Words Are Not Enough
47. They Have A Poet in The Family
48. Five Weeks Before the Wedding
49. Themes and Succession
50. A Case for Real Virtually

51. The Bus Pulled Away
52. Cookie Conspiracy
53. I Had to Decide Now
54. The Hokey Pokey
55. Between Two Worlds
56. Must Be Up to Something
57. Somewhere I Lost an Inch
58. Two Men and A Flapping Tarp
59. Lust Is A Must
60. Northwest Sunglasses
61. Starbucks Shortage
62. Is There Passage After Dusk?
63. He Must Be Up to Something
64. The Machine Don't Care
65. Give Her the Usual
66. She Died While Fixing Breakfast
67. Where Do You Go for Peace?
68. Before the Bonfire
69. Last Thing on My List
70. A Stranger's Goodbye
71. Your Teeth Are on The Counter
72. Things Take Up Residence
73. I'll Bet She Was A Nun
74. He Has A Drinker's Sunburn
75. The Unreachable Destination
76. The Night Pressed Around Her
77. Innuendo
78. A Closet Pillow Pounder
79. She Sees What She Imagines
80. The Red Box
81. Blue Edge of Darkness
82. White Moon of Winter

83. When I Ruled the World
84. She Tossed It
85. Attention Guests
86. The Best Laid Plans
87. Strewn Path of Unfinished Stories
88. Don't Get Comfortable
89. Gone Again
90. In Surreal Time
91. Evil Wicked Mean and Nasty
92. Whiskey Before Breakfast
93. Lost in The Page
94. The Elephant in The Room
95. Why Not
96. False Positive
97. Kelly Blue Book
98. Do You Know Who I Am
99. Bizarre Bazaar
100. I Just Thought You Should Know

– WORK SECTION 1–
Now Write Your Story

END – Wasn't hard, was it?

– FLASH 13 –

Gazing Out to Sea

The largest of all birds, I search for the Albatross. She is the flying symbol of good fortune as well as a significant burden. A life at sea was a long labor, rife with superstition and myth, the first forms of life insurance. Believed to be the soul of a lost sailor, the solitary bird soars far from land, traversing extreme distances over the endless oceans. An albatross flying with a ship is good fortune and to kill her is the curse of doom.

Few are called to the sea, but we all are called to create. Limitless as the horizon art emerges in a solitary, distinctive narrative. Depending on how the inspiration is answered, it can be both a rewarding commission and at the same time a millstone. Art is a vision wrapped in a struggle, venturing out, and praying for light. All humans want to build, yet many turn their back on the Albatross and produce a private deadweight. To ignore her is to slay the creative gift.

Playing ancient chants of insecurity in the background while fashioning my perfect dead albatross pendant I leave the musings of the universal to look at myself. I want, no, need to create something unique. I throw my misgivings into the sea, but they crawl from the briny and re-establish in my psyche. I turn my back on the negative as I stare at the blank page, and the Albatross whispers "write." Whining I have no talent, the Albatross answers "that doesn't matter, write." I have no inspiration, and she tells me "don't squawk, dream, write." I want to paint, and she says "write." She is my reminder that land may not be visible, but it is near, and with that knowledge, we both can take wing. Accepting the Albatross in her freest form is the gift from the universe. Genuine art is love and hard work, a crusade from a previous unknown assembling a unique genius. She celebrates my words so I will continue this expedition. It isn't over until we both rest on dry land, to prepare for the next journey.

– FLASH 14 –
Edge of the Alphabet

Slipping on the raggedy sweater, silencing the room with a flick of switches, I prepare for combat. Aching for privacy, yet needing collaboration, this writer faces the task. All the brilliant first lines quickly fade into a mumble as time and space are erased by the quest. Staring at a half a page of failed starts, I listen and struggle for the all-important second line which leads to the obliteration of the cursed white page.

The muse is personal and lives within, yet I beg for assistance to glimpse the truth. Pacing and scratching my deepest emotions onto paper, each story sculpted by keyboard and doubt. Mining a tiny whisper of inspiration, I labor in the hope of setting words aflame. Fact or fiction, romance or fantasy I try each form to salve the aching desire of expression.

With the limitation of language, I face unspoken questions and ponder life's fundamental puzzles. There is a yearning to expose the basest emotion and to describe it as a beautiful truth. Limited by 26 letters, commas, periods and a smattering of exclamation points. Daunted by the self-assigned task, I live as a hostage both night and day. I thrive on an imaginative threshold.

I am she who scribbles and erases, painting pictures with a script. I seek the edge of the alphabet working to the unexpected, as I stumble along an unmarked path. I pledge to spill my fragmented heart onto the battlefield of words eager to craft an exceptional story. Each effort emerges from my personal search for self. I write, with a simple purpose of one perfect sentence, the briefest combination of letters, to words, which develops a spark, to ignite a reader. My goal is for my effort to be read by strangers and then re-read by friends.

– FLASH 15 –

Life – Three Acts

Act One
Scene One
Welcome to the world, fabulous phenomenon. You are the cutest, smartest and most perfect baby ever. A bundle of infinite possibilities, wide open, thirsty for knowledge finding wonderment in all that surrounds you. They believe you will be president, cure illnesses and stop wars. Wrapped in pink or blue for the ride home, it all begins. You are so precious; the big people want to save your first poop in a pastel-colored album. Those same folks have plans for you, so be careful.

Scene two
You astonish everyone as you learn at an incredible pace. In no time at all, you are laughing and touching the world all within your reach. You make the soft squealy person so happy when you utter the sounds of ma-ma, and she sticks a bow on your head. The big loud guy loves it when you say dada, and he throws you into the air. You are pretty sure you can't fly, but he believes you will. The third word you learn is NO.

They seem so proud, as long as you go where they want after the approval, they build new rules every day. She talks about your cute little outfits, but you would rather not bother. The clothing is essential, pay attention; it is part of your facade.

Act two

The thought of school is frightening, but you are ready to go. Pencil box, tablet, and new clothes prepared as you run into the next act. Be sure that you have all of the accouterments of a proper pink or blue, "they" are watching. Telling stories, running, drawing, solving mysteries. If you don't fit, stop your worries; people who know nothing will convince your controversial self that you aren't good enough. Like a ship sailing around Humiliation Island you just want to fit-in and avoid crashing onto the rocks. So, bury pieces of your unique wonder deep inside, you will have time later. While you are at it, be sure answer the teachers with what they want to hear. You don't want to cause any trouble, and you need that grade. Here is hoping you are the genius they are looking for, because if you're not-well never mind.

Act three

Time has gone by so quickly. You married, worked, saved; you mastered the masks that meet your expectations of a society that doesn't always agree. As the conclusion of the final act approaches, you sit alone trying to inventory how it all happened. Wonder, just for a moment "If I didn't care so much about them, would I respect me now?" In this day and age, there are almost unlimited possibilities, but with that comes exaggerated expectations. No looking backward at the opportunities you missed or threw aside, those choices are lessons and funny stories, they can't change now.

In reality, you fulfilled a self-imposed role. No more pink or blue now you are wrapped in the invisibility of Ben Gay, but it isn't too late. You remember where your childhood brilliance is buried, pull out that fantastic self and strut it. "They" forgive the old almost as much as the young. You only have to influence one person to change the world. It's that easy.

Epilogue

Not Monday, or this weekend – today – write, sing, dance, and travel. Learn to yodel at the top of every mountain. Kick away self-doubt and fear then laugh at the memories. There is only one day that it is too late, and that is the last day.

– FLASH 16 –

Master of His Universe

Dad was a farmer and worked in the fields from dawn to dusk; but in reality, he was a magician of the heart. I was young when he built his "office" out of the shed by the barn. It only had one small window, too high to peek through and every winter we expected it all to collapse. He would steal away for minutes and sometimes an hour, never as long as he wanted. We knew he needed the creative time to survive. Every night just before bedtime, he would perform the most extraordinary stories punctuated with watercolors and leaping about the room. The evenings defined our lives and erased the isolation of the farm.

We never bothered him when he went into the shed. Momma said it was the least we could do for someone who loved us so well. As we grew older and were able to take over many of the chores, Dad spent more time painting and writing. Well into our teens we still looked forward to the extravagance of the stories at bedtime. As we children aged, Dad seemed to grow younger with the excitement of unbridled creation.

The years passed and the stories became more incredible. Dad was wholly involved in his private magical worlds. It was my brother Ned, who first noticed the steam escaping from the stove pipe on the roof of the raggedy shed. He used to say, "Well Daddy's cookin' now." I don't remember when or who first noticed the images in the smoke, but before long we could all see astonishing contraptions and animals that could only have come from faraway places and planets, a far reality of our home on the plains.

Not only we kids but Momma also became proficient in reading the smoky clues, this built anticipation for the evening performances. By the time Dad had to quit farming, he would stay in his office all day. Images flew through the sky and sometimes appeared almost solid. We would all imagine adventures inspired by the magic in the sky. We learned to take his work seriously, ever since the day a smoky pirate ship ran aground on the chicken coop and bonked my sister Lily. To this day she has a permanent part on the left side of her head, and she is an inch shorter. Everyone in the family was marked by Dad's brilliance; just Lily had proof.

Word got around, and people came on warm sunny days with picnic baskets and covered dishes for Momma. They would lay blankets in our yard and dream as the mirages floated past. One day a publisher visited and wanted to print some of Dad's work. Daddy sent him away, stating "it's not for me to decide. The stories belong to them." He turned back to the shed, begging an apology from the publisher; there was an idea demanding attention.

Momma had me race out to the man's car to stop him. Lucy, Doug and I are in negotiations for a new tractor.

– FLASH 17 –

It's the Trip

Five years of community college, $750 for the travel courses and Betsy finally scored the job of a lifetime. Everyone at Frommel's Travel home office was so welcoming, until today. She felt her nervous stomach clench when Mr. Frommel called her to his office for her first project. It was rare that he made the assignments and she replayed his words "This locus is out of this world."

What did Frommel think that she had a major in astrology? The only star she knew is the one you wish on, and Betsy had exhausted that joke in the first hours of the seven-month flight. Enumerable days passed as the tour of ultra-rich trophy hunters are catapulted towards Mars. With their constant demand, she tried to spin no cuisine, no old cities or gift shops into an experience. With a text marked urgent to the office, and she requested a souvenir cart to meet them at the Cape upon their return. She lectured everything she could find on Wikipedia, but as the time clicked by there are just so many constellations and black holes. Thank goodness for the science geeks and the NASA engineers, but even their jargon grew weary. The interplanetary group was cranky by the third week of the first flight. So, she started lesson groups; Mondays- Astrology, Tuesday-Poetry Slam, Wednesday-Star Trek, Generation me, Learn Klingon on Thursday, weightless disco/ cardio on Friday, and Saturday - mental health truth or dare. Sunday is free time when Betsy worked on her manuscript and updated her resume for Lonely Planet. She tried to thank Heaven for this opportunity as they passed through during the first week. This trip certainly sounded more exciting than the reality.

After months of night, they arrived at the Red Planet. There was a palpable fear as she listened to more technobabble. Disembarkation was exciting and luckily uneventful. They all celebrated the joy of walking on rubber legs. With camera in hand, Betsy felt the usual insecurity of being unprepared and foolish.

Mars, day one, she points out the sunrise, followed by the Ecosystem Manager and a package tour of the space station. Day two, an outing around the rock formation that looks like a giant head followed by a massive expanse of red dirt and an occasional pile of more rock; no sunbathing allowed. Day three, the space station farm and water processing plant with an opportunity to hoe. Once Betsy confirmed what they had been drinking she suggested preparations for the flight out. Mentally exhausted from eighteen-hour days of enthusiasm, Betsy missed every shade of green and Doritos.

Memo to Glenn Frommel, "Finished chapter titled Packing for a 14-month Flight and a Three-Day Tour. Suggest a guidebook only on this specialized destination as the International crew provides all of the information and instruction, which makes a tour guide as useful as boobs on a snake. The book will be ready for editing when we arrive in October. Do I get overtime? How about mileage?"

– FLASH 18 –

Bucket List

After decades of donations to the Ami du Louvre. Henry retired and felt it was time. More than a passion for art, he admitted it was an obsession. After two years of applications, Henry finally wrangled an invite to volunteer. Already a self-taught art historian he bought a French phrase book and a beret and checked off a once unfathomable dream from his bucket list.

Arriving two days early, Henry got busy, he found a place to say within walking distance, and he started familiarizing himself with the area near the museum. Finally, it was the day; Henry entered the Louvre for the first time. He had studied the layout and displays monitored the changing exhibitions and studied the classics since he was a boy. The magnitude of the entrance with the massive glass pyramid couldn't be lessened by his wet pant legs as he waded through the overflow of the river Seine.

He approached the guard near the entry and in his stumbling French. *"Pardonnez-moi, je suis un volontaire."*

The officer looked at him with panic in his eyes and answered in accented English, "Thank goodness,

I need you." He took Henry by the arm and pulled him towards a small group of people. *"Voici, Henri."* He then led the small assembly to a back hall with a massive nondescript door. The group of five started down the dark steps.

"SACRE BLEU!" The last three steps were submerged. The officer spoke both in French and English, "We need to move everything up the stairs. Gather everything you can."

"Let's make a bucket brigade!" shouted Henry.

The group answered him in unison, *"Excusez-moi?"*

He immediately got busy and placed the volunteers in a line from the floor up to the main level, as Henry and the guard began handing paintings, displays and marble carvings to the waiting volunteers. As the treasures started to pile onto the main floor, more volunteers appeared and extended the rescue team as the water rose. The growing and dedicated team passed caches of art and jewels hand to hand saving a shared history. They worked through the night, and when light reappeared on the gallery walls, exhausted strangers were sleeping together on the floor. As they arose, the people on the line were relieved. Henry never stopped, until the last painting of ancient gods moved to safety.

Henry and Jean-Paul, the security guard, faced a small locked door. "You know we must go in, do you have the key?"

The guard rifled through a large key ring, and nothing fit. They teamed together and pushed the door; it felt as if something was blocking their access. They counted and pushed, finally moving it just enough for Henry to squeeze through. The walls were discolored and dark. There was a single lite from behind innumerable bookshelves. Henry started handing out ancient scrolls and handwritten books. He focused on reaching the dim light; Henry was amazed at the wealth of art and literature some he recognized and some he didn't. It seemed like hours before he was able to make it to the light. Henry found a small woman as dusty and discolored as the walls. She was bent over a desk covered in stacks of canvas and paper, lit by the single candle.

The only sound was a quill scratching on paper and Henry's breath. *"Bonjour, madame. Je'suis Henri."* She looked up from her work and scanned the room. Henry wasn't sure she had heard him, he reached for his phrasebook, but it was soaked and unusable. *"Pardonne.* There is a flood, may I help you?"

The woman, scanned from left to right, still not speaking. He touched her frail shoulder and spoke again, *"Madame, je'suis Henri, et vous?"*

Her mouth opened and he heard a strange sound, like a grumble, and finally, she looked at him and spoke. Her reply was like a language he had never heard before, but he could understand when she spoke, *"Je suis Mme anonyme."*

"I am honored to meet you Ms. Anonymous. I'm familiar with some of your work."

– FLASH 19 –

Hemingway Walks into a Bar

There he stood outlined by the lights from the street, scanning the floor with his steel grey eyes. The cacophony of the room hushes just for a moment in time. I can see his jaw tighten, as his gaze comes back to me and he looks directly into my eyes. We hadn't met, but I knew he would be there that very night. As he approached, I was nervous, but I had planned on this moment since I read his first book. Ernest Hemingway walks into the bar and directly into my life.

His laugh was bold and full, but his gaze doesn't waver as he crosses the dance floor. He acts as if he was surprised to see me, but there was no question, I was the woman who drew his attention. His smell was all ink and adventure when he spoke, "Well hello beautiful; I haven't seen you here before." His voice booms with good humor. "Can I buy you a drink? Two daiquiris over here when you get a chance!"

"Papa. Little one, just call me Papa."

The door kicks open with a deafening slam. There he stands, a template for what we all believe a man to be. The room goes silent. Just as suddenly the energy raises and the crowd lights on fire. "I'm here," he bellows. "Let the festivities begin."

He charges the bar, and while standing just to the right of me he demands the usual, but the bartender has it already waiting for him. "Well, Martha, where have you been the past few years?"

I answer with all the moxie of a 1940s dame, "Reporting on the world Papa, and you?"

There he sits quietly in the corner, ink-stained hands wrapped around the fourth drink in a line of many. Stuffing scraps of paper into his vest pocket, he sullenly watches the activity in the room. The tinny music forms a background to the distracted writer. He is utterly alone in a bar full of wannabes. Our eyes meet, and he nods ever so slightly. He sits waiting for judgment as a character in his own story that the world believes it already knows.

Ernest Hemingway walks into the bar and the night explodes. Everyone's attention is drawn to the front of the room as a tiny roughhewn man speaks into the microphone. "Let the judging begin. We would like all of the Hemingways to come forward. There will not be a swimsuit competition this year." The room rocks with alcohol infused laughter.

Surrounded by 14 Ernest Hemingways playing the man to an extreme. This was the night that started with a crazy idea, but it has become a story of a lifetime. Papa won the Sloppy Joe's Hemingway Look-alike Contest. The fourth-place winner had a Santa Claus honorable mention.

The original was larger than life character whose persona has challenged his best books. The man has been gone for over 50 years, but Papa's spirit was everywhere that crazy night. I have been honored as the first Martha Gellhorn to attend the party, and my reward was way too many free drinks and six propositions.

"Next summer Bloomsday. Are you interested?"

– FLASH 20 –

Letter to the Author

December 28, 2013
Stephanie Meyers
c/o Twilight
Phoenix, AZ
www.Stepheniemeyer.com

Dear Steph:

I have been thinking about writing to you for a long time. Don't take me wrong; I'm glad that you brought me to life in 2003, but it is nearly 2014. You are my creator, and I am your alter ego, we are a very successful team. I just have a few questions.

You described me as intelligent, but holy cow, why am I so intrigued with a 109-year-old high school senior? The law of averages suggests that he should have accrued enough credits to graduate. I understand some difficulty with a subject or two, but he is still taking a full load of classes. Usually, if a guy is 20 and lurking around a high school, alarms go off, but not for Edward. Wasn't anyone in a supervisory position suspicious that he attended since the first Roosevelt administration?

I'm convinced that he loves me dearly, like a guardian angel. I admit you are right that only a teenage girl would go along with 1,651 pages of foreplay with a glittery bloodsucker on the PETA most wanted list. However, Steph, sneaking into my room to watch me sleep, that's creepy. You never mentioned the damp hand towels I found in the hamper. I spent over a year anticipating his magical appearances every time I stumbled, and you made sure I stumble frequently. That isn't protective, my dear author, to suggest this is romantic is irresponsible.

Why, why, why can I not be beautiful until some man consumes me? Your message to all adolescent virgins is that the epitome of passion is to wake-up battered and bruised from a possible wedding night scenario. Must lovemaking result in the physical destruction of a woman with a wunderkind tearing her asunder? Is this about your life? Really? My only chance of survival is to allow a stalker to suck the life force out of me, while his family salivates on the sideline. Please, girlfriend!

I recognize that my entire existence is about your ideal of love and life. The reason for this letter is to suggest that you do a couple of things for yourself. Number one, take a creative writing class and try to get those adverbs under control. Second, I wish you would consider some counseling.

You are right, the young have the capacity for intense emotions, but it has been over ten years, and I'm still an 18-year-old, high school graduate with an obsessive-compulsive, younger husband and a demon child. If I were more than a rant during a difficult time in your life, you would allow me to move to Bellingham, go to college and hang out with warm-bloods. I could build a life, and not be eternally tied.

Never mind, go on another book tour and buy more stock in Proactive. I'm not done with you yet.

With love and appreciation
Isabella Swan-Cullen

– FLASH 21 –

The Calling

In the pre-dawn morning, I hear a familiar voice telling me about her. Initially, it barely breaks into my consciousness, so I don't gather much information. I understand that there is a woman in trouble, big trouble. Wrapped securely in the warmth of my home, I can't appreciate why this would have anything to do with me. I let the message drift away.

Reading the morning paper, there she is again, this time with a picture. My mind races as I stare at her face. I try to decipher the significance and question why me? We live a world apart, and I'm confident we have never met. On no occasion have I been involved in anything similar, and I just don't understand. I must be overreacting.

I take a lunch break, and with my third cup of tea, I flip on the news. There is still a war, a theft, an accident and eventually the light news with literary time fillers begin. I return to my desk. As I step from the room, there is her name again. Just like a karmic dope slap, I'm in; I can't unhear the call.

Not sure what I can do, I put on my shoes and trust the answers will appear. No longer ignoring the pleas, I just go to the meeting place. I decide haste is never wise, so I sit to the side in the adjacent coffee shop and do a little reconnaissance. I hide behind another cup of warm invite and watch. I study the arrangement of the place, and it becomes clear that I'm not the only one that has answered. There is activity around a centrally located table, but many of the others seem hesitant to commit.

I leave the now tepid cup and work my way through the aisles to a display. I leisurely pick up a book trying to look nonchalant when the picture on the cover startles me. I made the right decision. I try to maintain some semblance of calm, poorly masking my excitement. I'm new to the protocol but already wholly involved in this caper.

As soon as I get to my car, I hungrily tear open the bag, remove the book and start to read. I consume each word, and the story awakens. Alone in my overheated Toyota, I bring Cecily to life. A book is just a compilation of markings on the page and a stylized cover until the reader gets involved. At this moment, I honor the hours of creativity, sweat, and faith as I devour the mysteries lost in the page.

– FLASH 22 –
Mystery of Night

A new job, a new town and within the year, Melonie's life had become all work and waiting to work. When the summer reruns appeared on television Melonie started a search for social interaction. Thanks to Meet-up.com she discovered a latch-hook group. Realizing she didn't need that many rugs, it was two meetings before she was searching again. While sitting in the deli she overheard a writers group sharing short stories. Mustering all of her courage she walked over and within minutes she was invited to sit down. Melonie never really thought about writing, but she was open to any possibility of creativity and friendships. Excited about the two-week homework of a 500 word flash fiction story based on magic she bought a composition notebook and a package of pens.

For a week and a half Melonie struggled with inspiration, false starts and deletions. With two days to go she put a note under her pillow, "Please give me inspiration."

The next morning, as she made the bed, Melonie realized the note didn't work. She searched for it, and it was gone. In its place she found the notebook.

With a sigh, Melonie shook her head assuming that she had dreamed everything. Moving the binder to the night table she saw the note sticking out and it flipped open. There was a message, "You are inspired daily, pay attention." Strange as it was, Melonie laughed at herself and went to work.

One day to go, and still no story. Melonie wrote a new note, "I'm listening," and went to sleep. It felt as if the night was only an hour long when she woke in the bright morning light. She rolled to look at the clock and found the notebook on her pillow. Melonie was sure that she had left it in her bag last night. It fell open to a story about a homeless boy and a raccoon, it was touching and a little funny. Melonie stared at the writing, and the script looked familiar.

The meeting was tonight, so she typed the story into her computer, expanded it and added a few multisyllable words. When she read it to the group they laughed and encouraged her to keep coming back.

From that day forward, Melonie would write a note before she slept, and awaken to stories of loss, humor, adventure, travel, and one Sci-Fi interspecies love story. The handwriting in the notebook was always her own; and it became more mature with every assignment. After months of mysterious tales, she realized the inspiration had always been there; she had turned her back to embrace a limited vision of adulthood. Now, Melonie doesn't need to leave notes, she's awakened to the amazement of her present world. She will never go back as stories fly from her awakened pen and she buys bundles of notebooks on clearance.

– FLASH 23 –

Too Much Magic

Pages of false starts, I search for an example, or a definition of magic. I confuse miracles with the sleight of hand that makes up my modern-day life. I lie on the floor in a sunbeam searching for the hook to start my writing. Frustrated, I flog my mind for the first desperate word, a sentence, a phrase. Hours pass and I reach out knowing the answer did not exist in my private closed world. In the agonizing search, I reach out to a like-minded writer on a late summer day. We walk in the beauty of the season to contemplate and discuss the questions magic poses.

Wandering through an art gallery, missing the magic when suddenly, I realize that talent and inspiration are miracles not magic at all. Studying sculptures of joy, and the pure colors shaping sunflowers, in light of day my realization slowly forms. It dawns on me that the freedom of dance and the personal soul-searching of literature are also miracles, but the final product is magic. The thought that Shakespeare didn't have a computer stops my reverie. As the day ends and I drive north on the interstate I hope, no believe, I have a key.

Before sleep, I place a tablet and pen beside the bed and ask for a dream, an angle, an answer. When

I awaken, the question has returned. I walk through my home and notice stacks of books, paintings on every wall and music playing on the radio. The realization that magic is in every moment of my existence blindsides me, like a downhill locomotive. I already live with magic; the only change was the need to describe it. As the sun rises and the darkness creeps to the corners of my office, I sit, still in pajamas wrapped in my writer's sweater wrestling with a spark of recognition. It is a miracle I want to write, but it is the magic I try to place on the page.

The lesson continues when I realize that eggs are miracles and egg salad is magic when I make my breakfast with two cups of tea. My semi-domesticated cat who chooses to live in my home is magic that she uses the litter box is a miracle. I dip it clean with new appreciation. Ducks flying through the sky and rest on a city lake is a miracle, curly-haired toddlers feeding them popcorn is poetry, another word for magic. Miracles are unexplainable magnificent gifts from the Universe. Magic-well sometimes it's a trick, other times an illusion but mostly it is an inspired step outside of reason. I thought there was too much magic, but now my eyes have opened. Dazzled by the spectacular show, I will never be the same. I rethink, and my gratitude grows without boundary. Now I will go to take a shower; the fact that I have hot, clean water shooting from the wall is a fantastic deception, but it is magic to me.

– FLASH 24 –

Trudging Toward the Horizon

According to Faulkner, "Writing a first draft is like trying to build a house in a strong wind." I am deep into a third novel, and I'm swept away. I stitch together five hundred words of fictions into a complete narrative. I reorganize, write, rewrite, and wrestle Mildred into a story with a plot and a reasonable end. If I cover ten pages, it is a successful day, and I earn the cup of the quality, English tea. This character lives with me, a woman older than myself, and she chatters during the day and late at night building her personal fiction.

Each night I beg the cosmos for inspiration, one clear thought. I doze and ponder a million possibilities. In the darkest hours, I awaken to throw my hands into the air speculating on what could be next scratching illegible notes on scraps of paper. What can she do to make the tale worth reading? A strangling fear arises, the story is improbable, and I'm stupid. Have I blundered in the wrong direction, wasting months and maybe years?

I work diligently, but in the past two weeks, the sun creeps into morning muttering a nagging list of three. I ignore the ideas, but they will neither fade nor quiet. I need an angle, a word, a twist of brilliance. I probe for anything to remove the clatter and release me to my manuscript.

Tonight, I must read for the writer's group, and a vision dogs me. The unmeasurable stretch of plains with bison herds so large they disappear into the horizon. The massive heads are grazing and raggedy hides soaking up the sun, preparing for winter. The heavy hooves trample with no need for socks, no use for sandals, feet perfected by the environment. I see them plod on, only rarely breaking into a stampede.

I present you with the apparition, and I feel released. I waste two more hours attempting to understand, trying to make the vision fit my story, and I realize it was never meant to, and I plod on in the driven herd of writers.

– WORK SECTION 2 –

Kickstarter Writer Prompts

**YOUR TURN –close your eyes and
PICK A NUMBER BETWEEN 101 AND 200**

101.   A Case for Real Virtually
102.   The Bus Pulled Away
103.   Cookie Conspiracy
104.   I Had to Decide Now
105.   The Hokey Pokey
106.   Between Two Worlds
107.   Must Be Up to Something
108.   Somewhere I Lost an Inch
109.   Two Men and A Flapping Tarp
110.   Lust Is A Must
111.   Northwest Sunglasses
112.   Starbucks Shortage
113.   Is There Passage After Dusk?
114.   He Must Be Up to Something
115.   The Machine Don't Care
116.   Give Her the Usual
117.   She Died While Fixing Breakfast
118.   Where Do You Go for Peace?
119.   Before the Bonfire

120. Last Thing on My List
121. A Stranger's Goodbye
122. Your Teeth Are on The Counter
123. Things Take Up Residence
124. I'll Bet She Was A Nun
125. He Has A Drinker's Sunburn
126. The Unreachable Destination
127. The Night Pressed Around Her
128. Innuendo
129. A Closet Pillow Pounder
130. She Sees What She Imagines
131. The Red Box
132. Blue Edge of Darkness
133. White Moon of Winter
134. When I Ruled the World
135. She Tossed It
136. Attention Guests
137. The Best Laid Plans
138. Strewn Path of Unfinished Stories
139. Don't Get Comfortable
140. Gone Again
141. In Surreal Time
142. Evil Wicked Mean and Nasty
143. Whiskey Before Breakfast
144. Lost in The Page
145. The Elephant in The Room
146. Why Not
147. False Positive
148. Kelly Blue Book
149. Do You Know Who I Am
150. Bizarre Bazaar
151. I Just Thought You Should Know

152.   Deep into The Mystic
153.   He Unfastened Her Mind in a Heartbeat of Time
154.   She Had A Horse's Face
155.   I'll Follow You into The Dark
156.   Last Words
157.   Omnimodus Interruptus
158.   Thanksgiving Night
159.   Harvest Moon
160.   She Let Her Hair Down
161.   Midnight Blue
162.   Hearing Voices
163.   A Moment of Yearning
164.   Dark Star Safari
165.   Last Call
166.   Is That Your Banjo
167.   Pines Piercing the Sky
168.   A Character's Letter to an Author
169.   The Art of The State
170.   After the Goldrush
171.   Sex After Sixty
172.   Watching Old People
173.   Here Be Dragons
174.   Blue Tongue Talking
175.   Sixty Days to Live
176.   She Couldn't Remove the Stain
177.   After the Snow Melted
178.   Some Time to Kill
179.   Languishing in A Cheap Motel
180.   Opera of Laughter
181.   Ice Follies
182.   Red Underwear

183. Here and Now Becomes the By and By
184. We Left Him in The Meat Case
185. I've Done That with Peanut Butter
186. Stone (D) Age
187. Suspenders and Short Pants
188. Bite Me
189. No Room Big Enough
190. It's My Nature
191. It's A Fine Establishment
192. The Trouble Started on The Freeway
193. White Flag
194. She Woke to Something She Never Wanted to See
195. Saturday Night Fish Fry
196. Stilettos and Silence
197. Dead Man's Curve
198. Dimes and A Nickel
199. The Stranger
200. A Terrain of Touch

– WORK SECTION 2 –

Now Write Your Story

_____

_____

END – Sometimes it's easy (but not often)

– FLASH 25 –

Delusions in Ink

It was over, done, fini. Shelley's career as a writer concluded today. She had always been confident of who she was. Ever since she was little, she made pictures and stories on lined paper with awkward block letters. Her mind, always fertile with tales of daring and adventure. Nevertheless, here she stood, finally admitting it was all a lie she told herself. Sure, Shelly bought the business cards, bookmarks, website and ads on Facebook. But with a 15-year class reunion approaching, she recognized that she was still a nobody. Shelly had made some flyers for the furniture store and a couple of daycare programs for the talent show, but not enough to make a living. This day was the moment she admitted to herself that she was ordinary.

The next morning, well after dawn, she stood up and left the nagging cursor of the computer and the screeching blank screen. Shelly's back turned on the emptiness, and she walked away from her failure. Now was the time, she gathered all of the instructional books and literary guides, and placed them in two boxes. Shelley conceded that she was not an illustrator but a woman, who could draw. Not the next great writer nor the genius of a new millennium, only Shelly.

Accepting the reality that she was and would always be just the receptionist at Broadwell, Tanner, and Dickenson. Shelly gave up her personal myth and confessed her name was not from the poet, but an actress on the 1960s Donna Reed show. It was a gallant fight with classes, submissions, and forays into e-publishing, but now it was over.

Backing her car to the drop off box at the second-hand store, relief washed over her. Shelly sat for a moment to release the delusion. All the humiliation and labor of a failed artist was over. A young man hauled away the boxes, and as she waited for the receipt. Being no fool, Shelly will use the donation tax break. She leaned against the fender of the car and watched it walk away; a little bottle of ink rolled towards her from the rear of the trunk.

Shelly picks it up and wonders why they called it India ink and remembered buying it at the craft store on Main Street. She noticed the lid is ever so slightly askew and she loosens it slightly. A dark mist, no, more of a shadow, oozed from the bottle. It rose before her eyes in an erotic dance, taunting her imagination. A private whisper encircled her, caressing her face and tangled through her hair. The inaudible moan was so sweet and yet, threatening. Shelly clutched the bottle as she climbed back into the car. "This ain't over yet." She pulled away on her way to the office supply store leaving the receipt behind.

– FLASH 26 –

Cheap at Half the Price (All prices should be adapted for inflation)

Times have changed, my grandmother earned $2 a week for her first job. In the mid-60s I made $1 an hour and was the highest paid kid in the park district. Today minimum wage guarantees a daily struggle with little hope of relief. Last Saturday, I used my debit card for a matinee and paid $5 for water. I cannot help but reminisce about my parents sending all four children to a movie with a dollar and four dimes for candy. Last week, I bought a pack of gum on sale for a buck fifty.

Nevertheless, if it is still a penny for my thoughts, this should be a bargain with inflation.

1.   I hope jeans never go out of style.
2.   Was Levi Strauss related to Johan Strauss; they were close in age?
3.   Would I be smarter if my brain wasn't full of trivia?
4.   Is Facebook an evil parasite that set on world domination? Am I just a pawn?

5. Working at a bookstore is probably not as amazing as I imagine.
6. Is the Dali Lama a virgin? If so, is it required in his line of work or is it a personal choice?
7. Why do many religions consider women to be not only weak but also all that is evil when they bring 97% of the casseroles?
8. I love to write, why do I work so hard at avoiding it?
9. Can anyone spell questionnaire right the first time?
10. Do I have days, weeks or years left? I'm going to regret the hours waiting for a program to open. (see #4).
11. Are all the radio and electronic waves pulsing around our earth for my entertainment and phone reception, bouncing off me or trucking straight on through?
12. Where has compassion gone? Is it out of style, or replaced by judgment and fear?
13. How hungry was the first person who ate an oyster?
14. When you receive your first AARP letter, you are already overdue for shredding or donating your bikinis and speedos.
15. If reptiles had fur, I would like them better.
16. Do any of my old loves still think about me, lovingly?
17. Hate takes up so much energy when indifference is the real opposite of love.

18. I'm sure Joan Rivers stuck to a comedy style too long.

19. I'm in the first generation raised on processed food; all genetic bets are off.

20. While on the subject, why are our food producers trying to kill us? That is not a sustainable business plan.

21. Even bad decisions often become historically significant, and if not, it will be a funny story.

22. We should begin a class action suit against the person who invented traffic circles.

23. Is there a chemical in the brain that gives talent, or does the gifted just utilize a part I neglected to activate?

24. Inspiration is just the coolest thing ever.

25. If you were a bird, would you fly high or just skitter around, keeping close to the earth?

You owe me two dimes and a nickel; payment may be made with in-kind ponderings or a direct deposit into my 401k.

– FLASH 27 –

The Stranger

Her career started when just a child. She was a liar; couldn't tell the truth when there was a better tale to spin. Fortunately, her mother gave her a tablet and said, "write that story down, and don't expect me to believe any of it." Now as an adult she has boxes of tablets, journals, and notebooks and in her adult years rewrote many of her wild narrations with fictional names.

One day, it happened, the stories went away. There was no trauma, no explanation they quietly withdrew. It was as if all creativity left the building with Elvis. The stories were who she was, so she struggled, then floundered. The only thoughts remaining were repeated old yarns with bigger words and the same endings.

One afternoon it was too much, as she agonized over a blank computer screen with a relentless flashing cursor. False starts and dead-ends filled the hours. She had a backspace for every keystroke. "I quit." She threw the mouse at the wall and slammed the door. Unsure how she found herself at a coffee shop, she blankly stood in line for a cup. Utterly, self-absorbed in self-criticism the hot coffee caressed her lips.

There was no notice as the cup slowly cooled in her hand as she stared in silence. Slowly a private conversation broke the blank meditation. They were too young to be in love, yet there they were staring at each other with more questions than answers. With the slightest turn, she saw a mother with three energetic boys. It was apparent the mother came in with a burning need to talk to someone who didn't sit on their knees. The young woman's face begged for an adult conversation and confirmation of her existence.

The cup turned cold as she hitchhiked on conversations, and inspiration manifested from every corner. The cold beverage was thrown in the trash as she rushed home with new stories.

The beginning of a secret identity took off. She considered the spying as research with a cookie. For week's she haunted the fringe of the coffee shop. To expand the search she dressed in black with sunglasses as the stranger identity expanded. Next, she tried new locations. Weeks later she traveled further and sat for hours in the rear of unique cafes and delis. Subsequently, it grew to buses, train stations, and biker bars. The bikers were very kind; assumed she was possibly unstable they offered a beer and a ride home.

Over time, the research continued to expand. She noticed the different reactions to outsiders from the periphery. The phenomenon moved her from stranger to strange. The casual style developed to layers of clothing and disheveled hair. The new personna was greeted with averted looks and judgment. Gaining skill in her study, she saw each identity created the public would assume a back-story for the unknown woman with searching eyes. On one special day, she scored $7.00 in change and two free cups of coffee. After the success, she took it a step further by adding a simple tin foil hat. The generosity ended adding, disgusted head shakes and mockery in its place. The research continued into being the other. She found a particular power in hiding behind cloth. In a burka, the foreign aspect of the unfamiliar brought pity from some, fear, and judgment from others. With a couple of snips and snappy accessories, she discovered it is possible to transform a burka into a nun's habit. The outfits were almost the same, but the reactions were not. It was clear her research was putting herself in the middle of the wealth of stories.

The last day of the month of pretense she removed a babushka went back to work. With pages of notes and a multitude of characters, situations, humor, and intrigue she returns to the office chair. Her unanticipated lesson was not the usual advice for writers of "butt in chair," however, sometimes inspiration comes from being part of the world.

Someday you may notice her quietly listening and watching. She could be any of the multitudes of the strangers sitting on the edge of society. Admittedly, she is not the only writer, and you may be someone's perfect inspiration. Watching, listening, riding, imagining a story, crafting brilliance you may not recognize.

– FLASH 28 –

Paper and Pen

To this day, I remember the first four pages of Fun with Dick and Jane. Before I started the fifth page, I recognized the miracle, "Okay, here we go. No turning back." And my life changed from moppet to reader. My junior year of high school in 1964 I read the list of banned books and fabricated my required English Lit book reports. Six years later, I immersed myself in the books I had faked and was stunned by what I missed and how I still earned Bs and Cs.

Now well over fifty years later I write. I make books, slowly and sometimes stumbling, but that is who I am. The acres of scrapped notes beg me to remember. They continually mock, whispering with infinite possibilities. Like a younger sister who knows way too much, forever taunting me into a fight.

The page once, and now the screen provokes a need to formulate letters and strokes to summon an emotion, to obliterate the pristine facade with possibilities. The blankness challenges toward a personal release of pain, love, and creativity. Characters who never existed in a day to day life whisper and call. The tales offer the possibility of laughter and healing.

The pen threw down the gauntlet of creativity. It hints of a secret trip to any place at any time caring nothing about history, gravity and possibility. It begs, no demands, a truth. The paper and pen are the tools that escalate the story, of an ache that demands to be soothed, edited and filled again? The blank page provokes every writer, to search the possibilities of imagination and storytelling while continuing to glare with a massive unblinking eye.

Everyone has a story to tell, but the clean white page tests and demands the writer to stop stalling, and spill out the last ember of resistance.

– FLASH 29 –

Possessed

The trouble started on the interstate. Brian had driven the commute for too many years; he rode with no thought or recognition. His existence had become up at dawn and out the door, sell insurance, lunch and sell some more. A new day same story, but this morning, during the numbness of routine, something changed. He pulled into the rest area he passed twice a day and parked in a shady spot. He rushed to open the company laptop, and the ritual changed. We might call it writing, but Brian felt he was a conduit for something bigger. For months there had been a story he mulled over on the long nights when sleep eluded him. This particular morning it erupted from his fingers until the laptop battery failed.

He drove to Centerville to find an electrical outlet and continued the marathon. He bought a breakfast that sat on the table untouched as he typed. This was an exceptional experience, and he was afraid it would continue and terrified it would end. He watched the cursor jump across the screen as words appeared in complete sentences. Brian understood the passion and frenzy of a dervish as he wrote the story of the man who lived vividly at the end of his fingers.

Hours passed, and someone from the fine establishment quietly removed the plates; he knew his welcome had worn thin. Brian hated the interruption and feared the drive to the office or home was too far, and he couldn't risk the time away from the pulsing screen. He stopped at a coffee shop, then a deli, and it was close to midnight when he inventoried three uneaten meals and an unknown quantity of coffee and tea. Brian pulled into his driveway and rushed to the dark house, laptop in hand. Brian was confident this was the most important day of his 40 plus years as he backed up the story to a thumb drive.

Two weeks passed, and the trance broke long enough to call the office. Mr. Timmons informed Brian that he was a full-time writer. It was made unquestionably clear he no longer sold insurance for Allstate. Brian hung up the phone and was elated. Brian looked at mounds of dirty cups and plates as he walked straight to the bathroom. After a long overdue shower, Brian had a new lease on life. As he dried, he felt the lure back to the folder pulsing on the desktop.

Later that day Brian momentarily allowed doubt and insecurity to creep into his reverie, but he soldiered on to re-read the manuscript. As he flipped through the pages, the fear subsided with a burning recognition that he couldn't own this narrative; it was too big for one man. Through his eyes, Brian re-experienced the ferocity of a genuinely original tale, and his passion renewed. He hit spell check with the satisfaction that even if he never wrote again, this would be his masterpiece.

Then a new idea started to whisper.

– FLASH 30 –

Right, Wrong and Sideways

Onomatopoeia – Is my favorite word. It's the term that refers to words whose pronunciation mimic the sound they describe. As Jackie Gleason once demonstrated, "Bam! Zoom! To the moon Alice." Of all the lessons in grade school, this was the one I- consciously remember most often. That day in the 50s is when it was confirmed that I love -words and the magic they can convey. All social animals communicate, from bees and ants to whales and apes. Our speech differs physically from the communication of other animals. The present science is that only humans have developed a language which is a set of prearranged signals. The jury is still out on porpoises and a couple chimps. It comes from a cortical speech center which does not respond instinctively but organizes sound and meaning rationally. It wasn't just the thumbs, but our manipulation of guttural utterances and huffs that built societies. We use the sounds to construct plays, books, history, and music.

When writing I search for words, the right ones. The ones that reach to the foundation of my message.

Often, I feel them in my brain, they form in the back of my tongue, but will not articulate. So, I keep a thesaurus within reach from the moment I face the page. After inspiration, and a writing device, the thesaurus is my most valued tool.

Flash fiction has provided a surprise self-imposed lesson. Telling a full story in five hundred words is a skill only developed by repetition. Learning the importance of the beginning, middle and end using so few words. It is necessary to involve the reader to create a complete story. Instead of a paragraph of description, I allow the reader to imagine and personally fill in details. I fight the urge to use a series of adjectives and adverbs describing when in reality, I require a better word. There is no need to elaborate with infinite detail when imagination can build a unique tale. The idea that my characters morph into who the reader needs is a thrill. When I started this challenge, my stories could have been double the length, but we had a rule. From that simple test, I learned to control the narrative and set it free.

Good writing is an exercise in research, stretching, and self-doubt. As I work to expand my vocabulary and build stronger stories, I celebrate words and the visions they create. I will continue to "bang and tap" away on the keyboard trying to evolve into a worthy wordsmith.

– FLASH 32 –

The Family Has a Poet

There are rules to poetry; they don't apply to many poets. Not limited to the dreamer who wrestles the mother tongue into beauty and angst bringing a tear to the reader's eye. It is a genetic flaw that causes the odd knucklehead to tell and retell a story until honed with an unexpected twist.

We must look into the heart of the poet to understand that every family has one.

The describer of lost causes, bringing a pen to paper or making the keyboard groan. Caged with a simplistic definition; they harbor a passion that must create for no other reason. They refuse to be limited by a thousand forms. So, with rhythm and rhyme, a song becomes eternal. Another will share a melody with a stretch and leap spinning that embodies the magnificent serenade. The painter of the soul composes in color and clay, to narrate a ballad in static form. The goal to etch life stories into an eternal design.

Your family has a poet.

A physical sonnet in the epic of sport adds grit to the expanding definition. The lyrical brilliance of impermanence celebrates the kitchen genius.

Encouraged past the limits of propriety a quip, with humor and sarcasm steps with the brilliant clown offering laughter to the human condition. The ingenuity of dirt carves romance from the cacophony of nature; nurturing a silent personal poem of the rose. The bard who had the improbable inspiration to slice a stone into brilliance and sets it into crowns. Only made more glorious the sparkling verse dazzles with the rhapsody of linen and lace. Everything that is done to fulfill the artisan's soul no matter how obscure is poetry.

You are the poem in a family of poets.

– FLASH 33 –

Don't Get Comfortable

Under my mattress is a pea
Just the smallest disturbance I could easily ignore.
Another mattress won't stop the irritation.
I roll to my side and lull to rest,
But my backside pursues the lump.
Just another middle of the night
Tossing and turning in the smallest hours
As the clock ticks 2- 3- 4.
The single legume harasses my calm
As I fail to command a quiet mind.
The pea yelps at my slumber, robbing my rest.
It begs for attention in the silence of the night.
It laughs as my mind, hurls ideas into the never.
Plots twist and are lost, songs never sung, paint dried
    in tubes.
A thousand answers to a hundred questions.
All lost to the murdering numbness of comfort.
Creativity is a pea, a tiny seed
Under my mattress and it nags like a bitch.
With a repeated turn of phrase
The subtle combination of sounds Seeking-Sea King
a whispered plot revelation bizarre.
I have a choice to curse or cultivate

to water the pea with my frustrated tears.
To bless one kernel to grow a thousand more
Wishing to feed a host of hungry minds.

– FLASH 34 –
After Dusk

Thousands of sunrises, bundled in brilliant color
This journey began before I could walk.
Full of promise for courage and work
Wasting hours with ribbons and curls
Trying to fit, where no one belongs.
Fleet of quip and slow of foot into the forest
Decades pass searching for a path.
A path only means someone has passed before.
Desperate to answer unstated questions
Stories without end gathered in a box.
Potential without talent
To fall in love, to enter history
As a multitude of dawns fade.
Into the heated noon and the dog days
There is a reward.
The passage to dusk
The time when all of the sins and mistakes
Become brilliant stories and lessons learned.
Dusk presents a brilliant gateway
To the mature beauty and gratitude.
Entering into the coolness of evening and rest.

– FLASH 35 –

3AM Saturday
(*My first prompt)

Standing here naked
Unprotected by clothes.
My foibles and failures
Completely exposed.
Childhood fantasies and hopes
Dashed and swept out to sea.
Still aching to identify
Of who, I agreed to be.
Collipe called during the lonesome storm
Commanding a penciled scheme.
Hone just one perfect line that's all to desire,
And encourage generations to dream.

Dare to Write in a Flash

– FLASH 36 –
Preheat to 425

Cutting butter into sifted flour measured by feel,
Baker envies the muse on card three by five.
Channeling a homesteader's lost culinary skill,
Hands move anxious with a primal drive.

Deftly rolling to line a geometric design.
Bursting with promise, fresh fruit with no flaw.
Hand full of spice no need for red wine
Marry to sweetness as pure as spring thaw.

Heating the wonder of nature's pure gifts
Perfection's aroma fills the home with a sigh.
Steam arms embrace by heaven's richest kiss.
Family wisdom tempts the heart's hungry eye.

The golden disk nests in a tin grandma sent.
Sliced while warm, no cream piled high.
The perfection guarantees the time to present,
An award for the first Pulitzer pie.

– FLASH 37 –
Run-Drop-Hide

Run. A knife maims, a bullet ruptures, poison chokes.
Drop. Words - the wounds you cannot see.
Cruel humor uttered in haste
Oral brutality slaps a shy face.
In silence, anger is swallowed to acceptance.
Absorb the humiliation and make it true.
Run, to the battle for self, the war is on.
Silence, depression, anxiety no more.
Search for a weapon to salve the lesion.
Hiding a bruised ego write on a slate.
A once silent writer unleashes to a page.
Hidden stories reopen the scar
Undrape the damage and poke with a pen.
To expose with the figurative.
Designing a bandage for the literal.
The choices and years slip away
And heal in the night to greet a new day.
All that is left is a fragment of bone
In the shape of a wish and a quill.
Life's cruel mist whisked away with the telling.
To the page a legend, a hero in real time,
Silence defeated in New Times Roman.
Another's remembrance we pray to acquit.

Life, trauma, death, starts with a whimper
To end in a tome.
Perseverance written into each name.

– WORK SECTION 3 –

Kickstarter Writer Prompts

You have just begun
Pick a number between 201 and 300

201.	Not for Publication
202.	Probable Homicide
203.	I Drew A Blank
204.	People Will Kill for That
205.	Self-Lubricating Years
206.	Jazz Music
207.	Gold Coin in The Sand
208.	A Different Species
209.	The Moment Everything Changed
210.	Reflection
211.	Insignificant Issues
212.	Ecstasy and Ink
213.	An Odd Group
214.	All In
215.	Fractured Dreams
216.	Folded Hands
217.	Furrowed Brow
218.	People's Problems Don't Bother Me
219.	I'm Behind on Everything

220. Mental Illness Runs in The Family
221. Dark Side of Cats
222. The Islands at The End of The Map
223. Unicorns and Rainbows
224. Boatswain's Pipe
225. Beneath the Floorboards
226. New Leaves
227. Honesty
228. Too Early for Dawn
229. Deep into The Misty Forest
230. The Last Thing He Saw
231. Swarm of Hornets
232. Pipe Bender
233. Past Tense
234. Race Course
235. Press Releases
236. Perfect Weather
237. The Top Down
238. A Waste of Life
239. Spontaneous Combustion
240. Hair Raising (Hare Raising)
241. Morning Star
242. The Pyramid on Ceres
243. Lost and Found
244. Off Limits
245. Blue Sleeves
246. Farmers Market
247. Pawnshop
248. Indispensable
249. Thoughts of A Crash Test Dummy
250. The Mysterious Note
251. I Can See This One Coming

252. 3rd Chapter
253. A Dip in The Lake
254. Water Flowed Over the Bridge
255. Coming of Age
256. Keep Running Find A Way Out
257. Into the Wind
258. Last Place to Haunt
259. Drivers Licenses and False Id's
260. 911 Fire Line
261. Pets and Stripes
262. Summer Surprise
263. Brother, Sister, Or Friend
264. The End of The Bridge
265. If You Want Time
266. Jinxed
267. Elvis
268. Flight Control
269. Cell Phone Next to The Tracks
270. Fallow Field
271. Crescent Moon
272. U-Turn
273. Power Outage
274. Flowers on The Window Sill
275. Cocker Spaniel Puppies for Sale.
276. Singing Alone
277. Vitamins
278. Tied Up with A Bow
279. Fishing in The Shallows
280. Chocolate and Cherries
281. Romance Unexpected
282. Spit Shine
283. Torn Warning Label

284. Duct Tape
285. Open the Envelope
286. Judgment
287. Grand Illusions
288. Stone Hammer
289. Tea Bag
290. Blue Moon
291. Leap Year
292. Mobile Pot
293. Persuasion
294. It Was A Close Thing
295. Left Over Chinese Food
296. Reincarnation
297. Ancient Finds from the Stone Age
298. The View Out of My Window
299. Muddy Shoes Everywhere
300. UPS Truck

BONUS – In case there weren't enough

301. Bossy Team Leader
302. A New Kind of Murder
303. Her Mind Went Blank,
304. He Held the Letter in His Hand,
305. Pools of Light, Rivulets of Shadow

– WORK SECTION 3 –

Now Write Your Story

You know the drill. It's your turn ↓
500 words or more/less

_____

_____

END – Proud of you – now keep going

Other works by Toni Kief

All available in the trunk of her car and on Amazon.com

Old Baggage
Novel
Mildred In Disguise With Diamonds
Novel
Mildred Romancing the Odds
Novel
Detours and Destination
Mostly fiction
Short stories
Detours and Transformations
Some exaggeration
Short stories

– About the Author –

Toni Kief never planned to write a book, until she was sixty. Born in the Midwest, lived in Florida, she presently calls the great Northwest home. She continues to resist writing an autobiography because of her odd incarnations and the tendency to catch a bus and leave town. Much of her creative energy goes into women of certain age. Toni calls her work OA, Old Adult, as she focuses on the ability to grab life full force and face unidentified dreams. Working with the Writers Cooperative of the Pacific Northwest, she has started her next book.

39163295R00083

Made in the USA
Middletown, DE
16 March 2019